Minecraft Short Stories:

A Collection of Minecraft Short Stories

By: Minecraft Books

DEDICATION

This book is dedicated to Minecraft enthusiasts and those parents who work tirelessly to get their children to read. We hope that by creating this novel, children everywhere will be excited to start reading!

LEGAL

Contents

The Wolf & the Zombie

Introduction

This book contains a variety of short stories showcasing various things that happen in the Minecraft world. These stories are filled with valuable lessons, funny experiences and entertaining stories. We hope you enjoy these stories and we encourage you to spread the word about this story book.

Chapter 1 – The Wolf Who Cried Wolf

Long ago in the rural villages of Minecraft, there lived an army of wolves and zombies. These wolves and zombies were great friends with one another, but they often liked to cause mayhem in one another's lives.

A specific group of friends loved to play practical jokes on one another at every opportunity they got. Two friends specifically – Kevin & Jared loved to prank one another.

Their parents always told them to stop with the pranking and to study more, but as you can see, they didn't listen to their parent's wishes. They continued to play practical joke after practical joke.

See Kevin was a zombie and Jared was a wolf. One day, Kevin had a fantastic idea for a prank he would play on Jared. They would always play outside in the jungle so he had an awesome idea.

Kevin would put on a scary costume before asking Jared to meet him in the jungle. They would find a secretive place so that he could scare the living crap out of Jared. Kevin planned and prepared for his big prank.

He put on a hideous creeper mask and hid behind a giant oak tree in the jungle. Meanwhile, Jared was excited to be playing with bows and arrows with his good buddy Kevin.

He got to the meeting place and couldn't seem to find Kevin anywhere. He yelled his name out and he quickly turned around to see if he could find him. Suddenly, he jumped back as he saw a large hideous creeper in front of him.

He didn't know it was Kevin and he was terrified. He began running around the jungle and Kevin chased after him. After 5 minutes, Jared fell to the floor and begged the creeper not to hurt him. He would only find that this mysterious creeper started pulling his mask off.

He quickly noticed that this 'creeper' was actually his good buddy Kevin pranking him once again. Jared burst out into tears while Kevin laughed hysterically because this was one of the most epic pranks he had pulled.

Jared laughed it off, but he vowed revenge against Kevin. He went home sad and began planning his big revenge idea. He decided to attend a sleepover at Kevin's house, which is where he would play his masterful prank.

While they were eating dinner, Jared said he would go to the well to grab some water very quickly. It was dark outside and suddenly Jared began yelling hysterically. Kevin dropped his plate and ran to see what was going on with his friend.

Nothing was wrong; Jared was just pulling a prank. Kevin laughed and slapped Jared upside the head for scaring him like that. As they went to sleep, Jared pretended to fall asleep but he had evil intentions in mind.

He snuck out the window and began yelling hysterically once again only to have Kevin waking up immediately sweating. He ran outside and again noticed Jared just sat on the grass laughing. He had pranked Kevin once again.

Kevin shook his head and said this wasn't funny anymore. They went back to sleep. It was almost 4 AM when an Enderman snuck in through their window and grabbed Jared. They had forgotten to close the window after their pranks and Jared was being wrestled away by an Enderman.

6

Jared yelled and yelled, but Kevin refused to get up. He heard the screams, but he assumed that Jared was just pulling another one of his 'hysterical' pranks, so he refused to get up. However, Jared was really in trouble.

Jared would never end up being found and Kevin was very sad to see his friend go. However, Kevin nor Jared were to blame for this mishap. They were both equally responsible for the actions that took place.

Don't be like Jared and be the boy who cried wolf. He cried and cried falsely, but when trouble really came – everyone ignored him because of his previous pranks.

Prank responsibly friends!

Chapter 2 – The Wicked Sisters

Long ago in the rural villages, there lived a young girl who received a lot of hate from older sisters. Her name was Crystal but she lived with her sisters who were very mean.

Her sisters treated her poorly and forced Crystal to do all their chores. She hated every minute of it, but she had no choice. Her parents were no longer living and her legal guardians – were her sisters.

She lived this life now for about 4 years and she was sick of it. One night, the sisters were all getting ready to go to the Village Ball. One lucky girl would have the opportunity to dance with Prince Herobrine who was coming from the Island to partake in this ball.

Crystal had never seen the prince before and her sisters weren't allowing her to do so this time. They left her to clean the kitchen and cook dinner, which meant she would not be able to go see the Prince. However, her sisters were getting ready and left for the ball.

The big night was here and she could hear her sisters joyfully laughing. They were so excited to go to this ball to have the opportunity to dance with the Prince. Meanwhile, Crystal was in the kitchen slaving away in disgust.

She was so upset. She wanted to go here, but because of her sisters, she couldn't go anywhere. She was tired of the unfair treatment she received all because she was young. She was sick and tired of it.

She decided to come up with a plan of her own. Crystal would "pretend" to work and slave away in the kitchen until her sisters left. Once they left, she would sneak into their room – dress up fancily and go to the big masquerade ball.

It was the perfect plan! She waited and waited until finally she heard the door shut. Her sisters had just left and now she was ready to get dressed. She rushed into her sister's room and put on a beautiful peach gown.

She grabbed a pair of beautiful crystal heels and put it on. From there, she put some makeup on her face and headed down to the ball. She had made just in time!

As she rushed there, she saw the Prince Herobrine high above her on a float. He was getting ready to make a selection. Herobrine wanted to pick one lucky girl to be his date for the night at the masquerade ball.

When he glazed eyes on Crystal, he was automatically in love. It was love at first sight. She was so beautiful and pure. She was in the perfect time at the right place just because she rushed to get in the view of Herobrine.

Surprising all the females, she selected Crystal. Her sisters were far back in the crowd and had no clue that the Prince had selected. Regardless, they were distraught with the decision because they each had wished they had selected.

Herobrine helped the beautiful Crystal on to his float and they began chatting. In just a few minutes, Crystal would have the opportunity of a lifetime. She would get to dance with the beautiful Prince in front of everyone in the village.

She was nervous, but extremely happy that her luck had permitted her this opportunity. The prince helped her down the float and they began walking into the masquerade ball. They would have the feature dance with the crowds surrounding them until they could dance themselves.

Suddenly, the sisters caught eye of who the girl was. They couldn't believe that it was Crystal and they immediately ran on to the main stage. They began grabbing Crystal and telling her to go home when the Prince screamed loudly.

He said, "Stop this minute! Where are you taking my lovely date?" The sisters halted and Crystal ran to the Prince. She began telling the Prince all about the sisters' wickedness which got the Prince thinking.

He said from this point forward, Crystal would live in his palace at the Island so that she wouldn't have to face the evil wrath of her sisters. Crystal cheered on excitedly while the sisters got pushed out of the ball by the crowd.

A loud shriek of boo's could be heard throughout the building as the sisters slowly walked out. They were in tears, but they got what they deserved.

Chapter 3 – The Village Love Story

While most zombies and wolves were friendly towards one another, there were many families that hated the other side. See, years ago – a huge war had waged between the zombies and wolves over disputed territory.

Most of the older generation individuals felt a dislike towards the other side. However, the younger generation liked everyone equally so it wasn't usually a problem.

There was a beautiful couple that resided in the village, but had to stay secretive. Joshua was part of the wolves and Anne was part of the zombies. Their families had both been involved in the war and had tremendous causalities.

Because of this, both families hated the other side. However, Joshua and Anne were deeply in love.

They had been dating for months now and they had amazing plans of getting married. However, their parents would kick them out of the village if they found out.

Thus, they kept it a secret but Joshua was getting sick of it. He said that love is precious and it should be far more important to their families than an old rivalry.

Both Joshua and Anne decided to tell their families about their love. However, Joshua said he would tell his parents first and only if they approved could Anne tell her parents.

Joshua went ahead and told his parents only to hear them yell at him. They demanded that he break up with this girl otherwise they will go and do it for them. They said Joshua was a disgrace to the family and he became very upset.

Anne couldn't see his hubby upset so she decided to take matters into her own hands. She decided to tell her parents. If she could convince her parents, she could send them to talk to Joshua's parents.

Her parents banish her from the household upon hearing the news and Anne becomes very sad. She runs away from home and begs Joshua to come with her. She says that their families will never understand.

Joshua and Anne pack their bags and decide to leave the village once and for all. They decide to find a cave by the volcanoes and lava where they can have their own secret hideout.

They plan to live there in survival mode until Joshua can find a job and make some money. Once he earns some money, they dream of living in the jungles in a beautiful tree house.

Joshua and Anne end up leaving, but their families never get a chance to say goodbye. Joshua and Anne end up disliking their families so much that they never reach out to them again.

The families both understand how much this relationship meant to their son/daughter. However, when they realize this, it is already too late. They have lost their children for good.

Minecraft Zombie Planet

Chapter 1 – Introduction

The year is 2040. Earth has been taken over by a breed of Minecraft Mobs that are explosive, vicious and brave. The human race is no longer existent and the world is controlled by ancient species.

The world is divided into three breeds. Mobs, zombies and protectors. The mobs and zombies are causing mayhem in the world with their evil-plans and although they do not see eye to eye on a lot of things, they both have the same goal. The protectors on the other hand are trying to protect the Earth.

The Overworld is the most sacred area on Earth, which is the small piece of land that is still controlled by the protectors. However, the zombies and mobs have been planning a massive attack on that area for years now. The protectors are weak and critically outnumbered, but they have heart.

The protectors are a group of heroic soldiers that aim to protect the Earth from the devastation that is soon to take place. The king also known as the almighty Jack is building up a team of Minecraftians that will help him protect the Earth. If this battle in the Overworld is lost, all hope of regaining their territory and pushing the mobs and zombies away will be gone.

This battle is a big deal and both sides know it. The underdogs coming in are the Protectors because it seems as if they don't stand a chance on paper. King Jack's greatest soldiers name is Arthur. He is in line to become a prince someday, but he is also the greatest swordsman alive. The protectors look to Arthur like a god hoping he can save them from their demise.

The zombies and mobs were filled with evil creatures who had taken over Earth coming from the Tundras and Dark Caves on Minecraft. They immediately wiped out the whole human race upon entering Earth. The humans weren't expecting such a massive group of unidentified species entering their world.

Using their explosive techniques and surprise attacks, they went on to defeat the human species one by one. Within a few short years, the world was now theirs. The protectors heard of this news and immediately rushed towards the Earth to stop this.

However, by the time they got there, it was too late. The protectors couldn't do anything as the mobs and zombies took over. They tried to keep a low profile blending themselves in with the zombies and mobs so that they wouldn't get assassinated.

Eventually after a few months, the zombies and mobs exactly knew who the protectors were. The protectors planned a surprise attack on a summer evening while the zombies and mobs were out partying. The most promising land in the planet was the Overworld area.

The overworld is a 20 mile city filled with diamonds, orbs and redstones that are extremely valuable. He who controls this area has the ability to keep peace on Earth and control the world. By doing so, they would have access to the most powerful resources in the world.

However, the tension over this area has been growing and the Protectors know that an attack is coming soon. Instead of waiting and getting attacked, they want to set up a fair and square battle with zombies and mobs so that both sides will have a fair shot.

King Jack has a meeting with the leaders of the mobs and zombies to discuss the details of this affair. If the zombies and mobs play fair for once, Jack and Arthur will need to pull off a miracle to defeat them. At least, they won't be surprised.

Chapter 2 – Arthur Meets The Zombies & Mobs

King Jack had his dispatchers send out a letter inviting the zombies and mobs to come to his palace for a grand meeting. He asked that they respect his wishes and keep things fair. He wanted to organize a battle between the two sides to determine it once and for all!

The zombies and mobs received the letter but thought hard and carefully about the proposal. Should they accept it? What if it was a trap? Why should they play fair? These are the thoughts that ran through their minds until Arthur made a surprise visit.

The Zombies and Mobs went into panic mode because they were terrified of Arthur since he was such a great swordsman. They became defensive but Arthur dropped his swords and told them to listen to him. He said this whole time they had come from the same place, but they were fighting like maniacs.

He tried to convince them to end the fight and to share the land, but the zombies and mobs laughed. They immediately began chuckling and ordered Arthur to get out of their area. Finally as Arthur was being escorted out, he asked them to fight fair and square.

He pleaded them to accept their invitation and to set up a fair battle if they were truly as strong as they said they were. The zombies and mobs felt challenged and immediately accepted it. They asked for the date when they would be welcome to King Jack's palace to talk out the details.

May 18th and 7 AM was the time the discussion would take place. The zombies and mobs immediately accepted and a discussion for the big battle was ready to go!

As May 18th came closer, King Jack had to protect his people. He and the protectors immediately began placing security measures just in case some hanky-panky went on inside his palace.

He had as many of the people as possible dress up in knight armor and they loaded up all the cannons. Various traps were set in exit doors just in case they wanted to pull some funny business. 7 AM hit and there was no sign of the zombies and mobs.

King Jack became nervous and asked Arthur to take some of the other soldiers and to go looking around. After about 30 minutes of searching, they had no signs of the zombies and mobs. King Jack immediately began thinking the worst and the palace was ordered to enter battle mode.

King Jack thought that the zombies and mobs weren't going to play fair after all their requests and they had to be careful. However, the mobs and zombies had just got lost on their way to the palace. They were actually planning to play fair but King Jack and Arthur did not know that.

They showed up 50 minutes late to the Palace completely unarmed. King Jack began hastily assuming something was up so had them all completely searched and sidelined. For once in their lives, the zombies and mobs were actually telling the truth. They had come to play and fight fairly!

King Jack and Arthur took the zombie and mob leaders into a secret room and they began discussing the terms of the deal. Both sides wanted to fight in their homeland, but neither could agree. Instead, they decided to fight in the abandoned deserts of Abo Rabi. They both agreed since neither of them owned that area and agreed to fight there.

The fight was set for 45 days from the day of the meeting and either side could use whatever tactic it wished for to win the battle. As the zombies and mobs left, they had a big smirk on their face.

Chapter 3 – The Big "Surprise"

After the big meeting, the zombies and mobs slowly left. Upon leaving, King Jack and Arthur let out of a big sigh of relief. They had managed to make it out alive without the zombies and mobs cheating or trying to get the upper-hand.

As they began to call a city meeting to discuss the battle that was soon to take place, one civilian from the Protectors noticed something strange. He said he found many strange crates or brown boxes lying around the city that wasn't there before the zombies and mobs came.

Arthur immediately began to inspect them when he suddenly started hearing a ticking sound. What could be in these boxes? He stabbed away at it with his swords, but nothing happened. The ticking only intensified until they soon learned that the zombies and mobs had hidden a bunch of TNT Explosives that were set to blow up their palace in 30 minutes.

Arthur ran to tell King Jack and they rallied up the troops. They grabbed as many of these crates as they could and headed it for the Masian Sea dumping these TNT explosives into the water.

With just seconds to spare, they got rid of the last crate filled with explosives and saved the city. King Jack and Arthur thanked the civilian and gave him a position in his highly esteemed court for a job well-done. Things were not about to get serious.

The zombies and mobs weren't going to play fair and they had done a great job tricking the Protectors otherwise. The zombies and mobs would have caused mayhem in the city and they thought that the Protectors wouldn't know who had done it.

Arthur wanted to head down to the zombies and mobs territory and start attacking them immediately. King Jack calmed him down and explained to him that they were severely outnumbered and the war technologies were far more advanced in their lands.

They had to think of a sneakier way to get back at them while winning the battle. King Jack made a profound statement saying that, "They may have won the first battle, but we will win the war."

They quietly devised a secretive plan for revenge while also preparing their troops for battle. They had a mysterious idea, but they told nobody. Only King Jack and Arthur knew about their ploy!

Chapter 4 – The Battle Begins

45 days passed and the war began with a big jolt. Cannons were shot from side to side and many

lives were lost. It was immediately noticeable that this war would be tough.

While Arthur was one of the best fighters on the Protectors side, they didn't want to unleash him on the zombies and mobs until the end. They wanted to protect him and his health so they let the soldiers, knights and civilians fight first.

The war waged on for a weeks and it became evident the protectors would soon lose. The blood, warfare and bloodshed was becoming too much to handle. King Jack called in his closest advisors and said it was time to execute their secret plan to perfect.

Arthur was the star of this plan and all of his advisors began crafting the plan. It seemed as if the war would not go their way and they needed to find an exit route. They would throw out the white flags and surrender the land to the zombies/mobs. However, they would make a request to them.

While the war was one-sided for the most part, many zombies and mobs had died throughout the process. The zombies and mobs accepted the white flag and ceased all fire towards the protectors. They decided to have a meeting to discuss the conditions of them surrendering.

The Protectors agreed to every clause that the zombies and mobs had asked for but one, they asked to have a small piece of land outside of the Overworld that their citizens could inhabit. The zombies and mobs decided to give them a small piece of land and agreed.

They made jokes and said that Arthur and Jack were lucky they weren't killed. King Jack was king no longer. Arthur and Jack seemed satisfied while the citizens under Jack protested. They didn't want to be ruled by the evil zombies and they begged for help.

It seemed like Jack and Arthur had a plan. They began building a monumental Herobrine Statue day in and out. After 2 weeks, the beautiful structure was built and it would house King Jack, Arthur and some of their best fighters.

This was the extravagant trap that they had been planning this whole time. They had a civilian from their city deliver this monumental statue packed with the guys inside to the gates of the Zombies and Mobs area. They looked at this status and marveled at it. They told the civilian to thank Jack and Arthur for this gift.

They rolled it inside their palace and let it sit there. Nightfall struck and all the zombies and mobs went to sleep. Arthur & Jack quietly snuck out and began creating hundreds of potions. These potions were a slimy blue-green color and were being made rapidly.

After having thousands of these potions stored away in their inventory, they began putting a drop on each and every zombie and mob that was sleeping in the city. They moved from city to city pouring this drop on each of them.

From there, they went to the Overworld to target the soldiers and kings of the new city they controlled. By morning, every single person through the whole city was now covered in this poisonous potion.

The result of this potion was that they would almost immediately be painlessly killed without making any noise. This was the smartest plan the Arthur & Jack could have ever devised.

By morning, no more wreckless zombies or mobs could be found throughout the cities. Earth was rid of these monstrous creatures and the Overworld was protected. The protectors now had no more worries of seeking refuge and hiding from zombies and mobs as they had won the war.

Jack laughed and said to his city, "They may have won the first two battles, but we won the war." The protectors lived happily ever after as a unified group from that day forward.

The Minecart Express

Living long ago, there was a man by the name of Paul who lived in a nice wooden house across from the villagers near the lake. Paul was an everyday journeyman. He loved to travel all across the large worlds of Minecraft hunting for something.

He never told any of his friends, family or neighbors why he kept journeying across the treacherous worlds of Minecraft. Unfortunately for Paul, he wasn't the best at defending himself. From mobs to monsters, he often got attacked and lost everything he had. While his parents were extremely wealthy, most of his inheritance was now lost just because he had trouble protecting it.

However, Paul never cared about money, fancy items or living in the most beautiful houses. He seemed to be consumed by something totally different. He was looking for something and he was determined to find it. But, what could it be?

One day Paul was journeying across the village when he realized he needed to cross a big body of water ahead of him. He was unsure of how he was going to do this because he had no vehicle to get around with.

It was a stormy night filled with rain and tons of mobs/monsters roaming around. For some reason, Paul was being more cautious than he usually was. However, Paul had something on his mind. He wanted to cross that body of water no matter what the scenario was.

He went through the village asking door to door if he could borrow a boat from any of the folks. However, most of the folks didn't answer the door or respectfully declined, as they were worried about trusting Paul in the middle of the night.

Finally, an old man answered. In minutes, you could tell he was an extremely wise fellow. He asked Paul to come in and made him tea. He asked Paul while he was in such a rush and why he couldn't wait until the morning to continue his journey. The old man even offered Paul a warm bed and warm meal if he was willing to wait until morning, but Paul refused.

The old man was extremely surprised. He thought Paul must be a criminal or that he must have looted someone. The old man asked him, "Son, have you done something bad? You can tell me. If you're on the run, I can help you hide."

Paul was not insulted at all and he quietly replied, "My parents are wealthy. I don't need to steal, I have enough – I need to go find someone."

The old man was still very confused, but he saw a look of determination on the face of Paul. The old man finally said, I'll get my coat and take you out on my boat. After many years, Paul finally showed a smile.

Paul replied by saying, "I graciously thank you for this and will look out for your well-being throughout." The old man laughed and went off to his room.

Meanwhile, Paul pulled out a map and began writing notes and drawing circles in random areas of his map. While it was very hard to see what he was really circling, it seemed like he was setting out the route for his big journey that he was about to take with the old man.

The old man finally got ready and they both walked out to the back of the house to grab the boat. The boat was a two-seater and it was quite old. It could also be told that the boat had not been used for years, as it was very dusty.

Paul wasn't the strongest guy, but you could see that he was working very hard to lift that boat up and carry the majority of the weight. He didn't want the old man to have to lift too much and the two men hauled the boat slowly to the dock.

At the dock, it was evident that they were not allowed to go sailing so late at night, but they disregarded all signs and gates. They hopped in the boat, filled it up with gas and they were on their way. Paul showed the old man the map and they immediately began routing their journey that way.

The old man kept trying to strike up conversation, but Paul was distracted. It seemed as if Paul could ONLY think about his trip and the mystery person he was looking for. However, the storm was starting to brew much harder and the trip was becoming tougher.

The old man saw an island coming up ahead and he suggested that they stop and wait for the storm to pass a bit before continuing. There was a lot of lightning, thunder and pouring rain, which made the conditions extremely difficult.

However, Paul refused and asked the old man to get off his own boat. He said, "If you can't handle the conditions, I will be happy to take you back home or leave you at the island. Let me take the boat – I will bring it back, I promise."

The old man now felt like he was being kidnapped and started becoming defensive. The old man wearily continued to agree, but was now beginning to lose trust in Paul. The old man started wondering if Paul was a psycho or going to harm him in any way.

The journey continued and it seemed to be a lot farther than either of the two expected. The sun was starting to peak out of the sky and the storm was also slowing down. Paul and the old man were hungry, thirsty and sleepy but they refused to stop to service any of their needs.

Paul was more determined than ever and he took the helm of the boat from the old man. He was pushing the boat to its limits, as he wanted to reach the end of his destination as soon as possible. After a few more hours of continuing through the rocky waters, they seemingly ended up on the big circle that was marked on the map.

The old man in his all years had never seen such a sight. It was an abandoned island filled with bats and tiny little caves. He was wondering why on earth Paul wanted to come out here. There was nothing here and now the old man became extremely worried his kindness was going to kill him.

The old man started feeling like his life was in danger and that he was going to be kidnapped. However, Paul seemed disinterested in even talking to the old man. The old man asked him an array of questions, all of which Paul just ignored.

Paul just kept pushing forward, digging in random areas and continued to act like he was looking for something or someone. Finally the old man grabbed Paul by the shoulders and said, "Son what are you doing out here? What could you be looking for? Tell me, I can help you!"

Through his young life, Paul obviously didn't have many friends. Paul began seeing from all of the actions of the old man, that the old man actually cared about him. The old man was the closest thing to a friend Paul has had in many years and Paul finally started making that realization.

Paul decided that it was unfair to keep the old man under the radar for much longer so he sat him down on a rock and started talking to him. Paul said, "I apologize for ignoring you and not being as kind to you as you have been to me. I have been on a mission to find someone for the last 5 years and have not been able to find him."

Paul continued, "I overheard my neighbors talking last night that this person will be here in the abandoned island so I had to find a way to come here. I really thank you for lending me the boat and coming with me, if you don't want to continue – I completely understand. You can even take the boat with you, I'll find my way back somehow."

The old man just gazed away at Paul. The old man was trying to understand everything that Paul had just told him, but he began to comprehend a lot more. The old man replied by saying, "Nonsense son. I will stick with you till the end and we will go back home on my boat in triumph! You must tell me though who this mysterious person you are chasing is and what he has done to you."

Paul continued to seem hesitant in telling the old man whom he was chasing. However, the old man was persistent. Paul could tell how stubborn the old man was and this was the first person in years who had cared about Paul. He broke out in tears and started telling the old man everything.

Paul franticly started saying, "I'm chasing someone known as the Herobrine. He's one of the hardest people in all of Minecraft to find, but he has done some very bad things to my family. When I was born, he kidnapped my mother and left me on the steps of a random house. I spent the first few years of my life being raised by a family that wasn't my own until my father finally found me and rescued me."

Paul continued his story sobbing hysterically, "I have never seen my mom and it's all Herobrine's fault. I want to find him so I can cause him the same sort of pain and misery he has caused me and I will dedicate my whole life to make him suffer."

The old man comforted Paul as it made a lot of sense now. Paul wasn't a psycho or some insane person, he was just deeply hurt. He wanted revenge on the person who had taken his mother away from him. The old man now understood and he was more ready than ever to make sure Paul got the vengeance he deserved.

They began devising a plan of how they would break down the island. The island was a rather large island and even though everything was abandoned, they had to find a safe strategy to find the Herobrine. The island was filled with tons of dark caves and forests, but Paul seemed convince that the Herobrine would be hiding somewhere in the caves.

Paul and the old man began devising a plan together. They knew that some caves were inhabitable so they were going to split up and cut some trees up and put wooden logs in front of each cave that they were sure Herobrine could not be in.

47

The two split up and agreed to meet up before sundown at the rock where they had the big talk. Paul went north and the old man south with a handful of logs. They went cave to cave peaking their heads inside and taking a good look.

If there were no torches and no signs of life, they immediately put a log on that cave. Even footprints were a good way to know if someone had been near the cave in quite a while.

There were hundreds and hundreds of caves all over the deserted island. They both slaved away looking and looking. Finally after searching through hundreds of caves, both of them met back right before sun down at the special rock.

The old man reported that after searching through hundreds of caves, only 4 potential caves could be inhibiting the Herobrine. Paul smiled excitedly as this meant that weren't too many caves to search from as he had only 3 potential caves where someone had been recently.

They knew this invasion was perfect to do at night so that they could catch Herobrine by surprise, so they decided to take a break by eating and napping. The old man caught some fish and cooked it before they both found a nice tree to nap on.

They agreed to wake up in 3-4 hours so that they could both get up and prepare their invasion of the caves to find Heobrine. They ate, laughed and napped. Before they knew it, 3 hours had passed and Paul jumped awake.

Paul ran to the old man shaking him rapidly waking him up in excitement. This was the moment Paul had been waiting for all his life. They got their items together and rushed towards each of the caves slowly and quietly.

Paul and the old man decided to start with the caves at the north-most point of the map. The first cave was way too small for the Herobrine to be inside so they immediately decided to mark that one off. The second cave was only 500-600 feet long and they went through the whole thing to find that nobody was inside of it.

They were down to 5 more potential caves. After getting a good understanding of the potential caves, there were 2 left on their long list. They decided to start with the biggest cave with the most ground to cover and Paul decided to lead the way.

They spent a few hours going from toe to toe on the cave only to realize that the Herobrine was not in this cave. Paul ran out of the cave with his torches, as this must have meant that the Herobrine was resting in the latter cave.

The old man was tired, but he knew how much this meant to Paul so he continued onwards with him. They rushed to the other cave and began very slowly searching every bit of the cave. This cave wasn't as big as the other cave, but it had many different rooms inside making it tougher to explore than the last one.

After exploring every last bit of it, they couldn't find anyone. Paul slouched to the floor as he was extremely disheartened by this news. The old man tried comforting him and they both thought the information they had received from Paul's neighbor wasn't very accurate.

Paul began sobbing hysterically as this was the closest he felt to the Herobrine in years and this whole journey was a waste. Paul felt bad that he had took the old man this far and they weren't able to achieve their goal.

However, the old man picked up Paul and told him to stop slouching around. He said that he shouldn't give up this easily and maybe there's some sort of secret door inside one of these caves that may lead to the Herobrine. Paul felt like the old man was just trying to comfort him so he began ignoring his advice.

The old man however did not stop as he continued to bang on every part of the cave until finally he hit something. Suddenly he noticed that one of the walls in the cave were scraping off. He started scraping it off using a large boulder and Paul still continued to seem disinterested, but the old man thought he was on to something.He was correct! After scraping the walls of the cave, it read an inscription, which represented a set of coordinates. They were coordinates on the map and the old man grabbed the map from Paul. The coordinates pointed somewhere very close and it happened to be inside the cave.

Paul and the old man started pushing towards the coordinates and they quickly found another wall. However, they scraped this wall and nothing happened. Paul became very frustrated as this seemed to be a cruel joke.

Paul out of pure frustration began banging on the wall with the coordinates when something magical happened. The doors of the cave walls opened and a Minecart showed up. The old man and Paul looked at the Minecart in disbelief as they had never seen anything like this in the past.

They hopped on the Minecart only to find the walls behind them closing while they rode the Minecart down this hidden shaft. There were boxes, crates and TNT all over around the cave while the journey seemed to take quite a while. Finally after a few minutes of going through the Mincart, they reached the end and the Minecart stopped. There was a nice wooden door with glass panes and it looked like this was someone's house.

They tiptoed through the house and quickly found a lavish house. Filled with televisions and beautiful beds, this house belonged to someone very wealthy. But, what was it doing hidden in an abandoned island at the very bottom of a cave?

Paul began franticly exploring the house when he came across Herobrine sleeping peacefully in his bed. This was his opportunity to kill Herobrine, make him suffer or seriously hurt him. Paul pulled out his pickaxe and sword, but as much as he tried to strike Herobrine, he simply couldn't do it.

What was wrong? Why could he not strike Herobrine, the man who had caused so much torture and turmoil in his life? Suddenly, Herobrine began moving and he opened his eyes. He looked up and saw Paul and he immediately knew who he was. He fell out of his bed and jumped into his drawer to grab his own sword.

He started yelling at Paul and asked him, "What are you doing? Who are you? Why are you in my house, I will kill you." He then began yelling, "Mobs – invasion! An invasion is taking place, help me NOW!"

However, the old man was waiting outside the room with a TNT box that he had picked up while riding on the Mincart on the way down. He warned the mobs and everyone else around him that he would not hesitate to blow up the TNT, which would then kill them and everyone around him.

They backed away and the old man told them to take the Minecart and leave, as they didn't need to get hurt over mistakes that were made by the old man. They obliged to what the old man had to say and immediately hopped on the Minecart and began leaving the premises.

Paul in the meantime was in a standoff with the Herobrine. They both had their swords thrusting towards each other, but they both seemed fearful of hitting one another. Finally, the Herobrine started begging Paul to put his sword down and that he had an explanation for everything he did.

Paul refused to listen to a word he said and all he kept yelling was, "Where is my mother? What did you do to her?" However, Herobrine refused to answer the question and he kept telling Paul to calm down and to put his sword down. He kept saying that Paul had to listen to what happened, but Paul refused to hear him out.

Paul finally gave the Herobrine an ultimatum. You must either give me my mother or I will kill you right here. The Herobrine replied saying that he hadn't seen his mother in years and without one more word, Paul took his sword and repeatedly stabbed the Herobrine in the head.

From there, Paul walked out of Herobrine's room and told the old man that he had accomplished his goals. They were ready to take the Minecart back up to the caves so that they could finally go home. This was an insane last few days and it was now time for them to live their own lives.

They sailed back home and Paul thanked the old man graciously for his efforts and help with all of this before they went their separate ways.

THE END.

Minecraft Invasion Part I

Prologue:

Minecraft is a game where people from all walks of life can come together and unleash their creativity.

In today's world, many people's imagination becomes restricted because of a few key factors. These factors can include rules, parents, other forms of authority, and of course – reality.

What separates a child from an adult? Adults are familiar with all these factors, thus their imaginations are crippled. Young children who are not as familiar with all these factors are seen expressing their imagination and dreams every day.

When you ask a child what they want to be when they grow up, they will respond with something like, "I want to be an astronaut!" Other kids might say, "I want to be a king!" or

"I want to be a soccer player!"

"I want to be a singer!" Or my favorite,

"I want to be a royal astronaut playing soccer and singing in space!"

When you ask an adult what they want to be when they grow up, they will respond saying something like, "I'm already grown, I can't be a royal astronaut playing soccer and singing in space."

Unfortunately, adults tend to give up the essence of reality and stop letting their imaginations run free.

On the game Minecraft, adults and children can BOTH express a keen sense of creativity and imagination. Neither is crippled by the limitations of *reality*.

This story is about the invasion of imagination in Minecraft and how a group of unhappy, restricted individuals learn to once again be creative as they enter the world of Minecraft.

Part I:

RING, RING, RING. Jeff's alarm pounded, notifying him that it was six o'clock in the morning. Unable to deal with the reality, he hit the snooze and slapped his phone to the floor.

A couple of minutes later he noticed the bright, round, yellow sun peeking its way through the gap in his blinds. The several missing blinds hanging in front of his small glass window allowed all the light of the world to shine in and awaken him from his deep slumber.

Grumpy and half dazed, Jeff rose out of bed like a zombie. His movements were slow and his eyes looked like he wasn't even there.

He continued with his daily routine. After struggling out of bed, he made his way to the bathroom. As he turned the light on, the luminance reflected on the bare white walls and made him cringe. He turned them back off and proceeded to the sink. He fumbled around searching for his toothbrush in the darkness.

"Ouch!" He shrieked as he stubbed his toe on the edge of a cabinet. He slammed his hand down in frustration only to find his toothbrush. Now broken into two pieces, he picked up the end with the brush and ran it under the faucet.

Luckily for Jeff the toothpaste was always in the same place, in the first drawer to the left. He squeezed some onto his brush and began cleaning his teeth. He washed his face and got into the shower.

He let the water run and stood under the warm sensation for a few minutes while he let his mind wander. He thought about what it would be like to have a house he actually liked and wake up to something other than the view of the neon sun and the backside of another brick building. He thought about what it would be like to be able to fly, to spend his days doing something fun rather than going to work.

The hot water suddenly ran out and the coldness snapped Jeff back to reality. He jumped out of the shower, dried off, and went to his closet.

Pants, shirts, more pants, more plain solid colored shirts. He grabbed the first pair without thinking much of it and got dressed.

He looked in the mirror. Ordinary haircut, ordinary face, ordinary outfit, and ordinary attitude. He predicted it would be an ordinary day, so he grabbed his ordinary briefcase and headed out the door.

Jeff was a salesman. He would go knocking door to door and try to sell magazines. Ordinary magazines.

After leaving his building, he walked to the bus and took it thirty six miles away to the city. He got off the bus and waved goodbye to Don, the bus driver who he had gotten to know over the course of three years in the sales world.

He stepped off the bus expecting nothing out of the ordinary to happen. Knock on a few doors, get ignored, get ushered away, or worse, see someone through a window who was pretending to be away. That was the ordinary day that Jeff was expecting.

Jeff continued walking down a row of houses until he reached the end. That house would be his first stop. He walked to the front door and rang the doorbell. One minute passed, then another, and another. After five minutes of waiting, he breathed a disheartened sign and began walking down the stairs.

Out of nowhere, Jeff heard an explosion. Use to his ordinary rejection and nothing more, he was startled by the thunderous noise that seemed to be coming from the backyard.

Worried that someone might be injured, he cautiously made his way to the back of the house where a fence stood in between him and the location of the blast. Being of ordinary height, Jeff could not see over the fence. Being of ordinary strength, Jeff could not jump over the fence.

"Is… Is anyone thh-there?" He stuttered.

No one replied and Jeff shrugged and began walking away when suddenly, *BANG!* Another explosion burst behind him.

65

"Is... Is anyone there?" He said this time, slightly more nervous.

No one answered his again and he turned to walk away when a little boy appeared directly behind him. "AH!" shrieked Jeff.

The little boy had given Jeff a quite a startle. Unsure what to say or do, Jeff's instinct resulted in him asking, "Are you parents home? Do you want to buy a magazine?"

"Yep and sure mister! What kinda magazine you got?!" the child responded with excitement.

"Well I have sports, fashion, games…"

"What kinda games? Computer games? Video games?" interrupted the child.

Jeff flipped through the magazine. In all his years as a salesmen, he has never bothered to read the magazines that he was actually selling.

"There's Pokémon, Batman, Neopets, WWE, Mine…"

"MINECRAFT? Lemme see, lemme see!" he plucked the magazine out of Jeff's hand and began looking for the section concerning Minecraft.

"THIS IS SO COOL, SIR! Minecraft is my favorite game! Do you play it? It's super fun and awesome!"

Jeff had never heard of Minecraft. Little did he know that this day would change his life forever.

"Oh… No I've never heard or played it before." Jeff replied in shame. Even though he had only known this kid for five minutes, he immediately didn't want the kid to think he was… *lame*.

"NO WAY! Okay you have to check it out. LIKE NOW! Follow me!"

Confused but curious, Jeff followed the boy to the backyard, the site of the explosion.

"My names Alex, by the way! What's yours?" The boy said as the made their way to a little shed in the yard.

"I'm Jeff."

"Okay, Jeff. I'm about to show you the coolest thing ever, but first I need to know something. Can you keep a secret?" Alex's big blue eyes expanded and stared at Jeff.

"Sure..." Jeff said hesitantly.

"Good enough for me!" replied Alex, "Okay, so this is the beauty! Minecraft!"

Removing a thin blanket, Alex revealed a large computer screen, a giant speaker system, and most interestingly, something that looked like a *portal*.

"What is all this?" Jeff asked in confusion.

"This is my portal machine. I've been working on it for a while now." Alex then lowered his voice to a low whisper, "It can teleport you into the game."

Jeff was beyond mystified. He was wondering what was wrong with Alex. *You can't teleport; that is impossible,* he thought.

"I know it sounds crazy, but it works! There are just a few bugs I need to work out." Alex replied as if he was expecting Jeff to show disbelief, "Let me show you!"

Alex pushed a button. The screen lit up, the speakers hummed a tune, and most interestingly, the portal began to glow.

"Whoa." Jeff said in awe.

"Wanna make your own character to be in the game?" Alex asked courteously.

"Sure…" Jeff replied, still in shock.

Alex walked Jeff through the process of creating his own Minecraft character. Jeff began by making his character ordinary when Alex interrupted, "Why don't you make him look taller and stuff?"

The first model Jeff made looked like a cubed version of himself. It has an ordinary haircut, an ordinary face, an ordinary height, and overall it was ordinary.

Alex saw Jeff struggling, "Jeff! You're missing the point. Minecraft isn't just about making another you. It's about making a cooler, more creative version of you. The best part of the game is being able to do ANYTHING!"

With Alex's little spiel, Jeff decided to try making his character again. This time, Alex gave him access to *skins*. These skins were amazing. You could be anything or look like anyone.

"What do you wanna be when you grow up?" Alex asked.

"I'm already grown up."

"Oh, so you wanted to be a magazine seller?

"No…" Jeff had the ashamed look on his face and put his head down.

"Then what do you wanna be, man?"

"I want to be an astronaut!" Jeff said, finally cracking a smile. Then he realized that was impossible, "Just kidding, that's impossible." His smile transformed into a frown.

"Nothing is impossible, at least not on Minecraft!" With a few master clicks, drags, and selections, Alex downloaded an astronaut skin for Jeff.

"Done. There you go astronaut Jeff!"

A little spark inside Jeff lit up. His stomach was turning with excitement. He had never felt this way, not since he was a little kid and it was Christmas morning.

Embarrassed at his enthusiasm for a game, Jeff hid his grin.

"Cool." He replied as he tried to mask his overwhelming excitement.

"Okay now let me show you creative mode! It's the best!"

Creative? That was a word that wasn't too familiar to Jeff. The most creative thing he had done was picking out the clothes in his closet.

With a few clicks and clacks, Alex placed Jeff into the creative world of Minecraft. The two spent hours exploring and building cool things. Alex shows Jeff everything from the Empire State Building to the Arc de Triomphe. In just a few hours, the two had traveled and flown across the world.

Jeff looked at his watch. Ten o'clock it read.

"Oh, I have to leave now. The last bus is leaving soon."

"Aww, okay! Come back tomorrow, I have the best part to show you tomorrow! It's called survival mode."

The two new friends said goodbye and parted there ways.

On his way to the bus, Jeff's mind was filled with thoughts of cube shaped grass, stone, wool, meat, and structures. Before he knew it he was on the bus.

"Hey Jeff, how was your day today man?" asked Don the bus driver.

"Good! Met a really cool kid named Alex, and he showed me this game called Minecraft!"

Don scrunched up his face and made a strange noise while muttering something under his breath.

"What was that, Don?" Jeff asked innocently.

"Oh, nothing! Just something in my throat, man" Don said/

Jeff, tired from a long day of using his brain to think outside of the box, fell asleep in the bus. His mind wandered from extravagantly designed homes on Minecraft to spaceships headed to outer space.

Forty-five minutes later, Jeff felt a hand on his shoulder.

"We're here man." Don said.

"Oh, okay." Jeff got up and handed Don the bus fair, "See you tomorrow."

RING, RING, RING. Jeff's alarm sounded as it did the morning before. It was once again six o'clock in the morning. Instead of slapping his phone to the floor, Jeff turned his alarm off and pushed his blinds away. He opened the window and took a whiff of fresh air.

He then noticed the golden sun greeting him as he awoke from his pleasant slumber.

Not the slightest bit grumpy or dazed, Jeff rose out of bed as if he was floating on cloud nine.

He continued with his daily routine, only it was slightly less ordinary. After floating out of bed, he made his way to the bathroom. As he turned the light on, the luminance reflected on the bright white walls and made him grin. He left them on and proceeded to the sink.

He reached in the bottom cabinet and grabbed a new, unbroken toothbrush. He grabbed the toothpaste and squeezes it gently onto the brush. Cleaning his teeth and glaring at himself in the mirror, he smiled.

He washed his face and walked into the shower. He let the water run for a couple of minutes, and for the first time in years he did not imagine his life any different that it was today.

He dried off and walked over to his closet. Instead of looking at everything as it appeared the day before, he looked at his wardrobe with a new eye. It was not simply a collection of pants, shirts, more pants, and more plain solid colored shirts. Instead, it was a collection of a blank canvas. He grabbed a green t-shirt and a nice blue pair of jeans. He got dressed without feeling as if it was a habitual drag.

After getting into his clothes, he headed to the mirror of judgment. However, things would be slightly different today. He grabbed the gel out of his drawer and styled his hair. He used soap to wash his face. He sprayed the cologne he had got for a gift a few months ago. He looked in the mirror in the brightly lit bathroom. Extraordinary hair, extraordinary face, extraordinary outfit, and most importantly, an extraordinary attitude.

He predicted it would be an extraordinary day, so he left his ordinary briefcase at home and took with him one magazine. The magazine of Minecraft.

After leaving his building, he hustled to the bus and took it thirty six miles away to the Alex's house. For some reason, Don wasn't the driver today. Confused but too excited to think much of it, Jeff closed his eyes and imagined flying over the Arc de Triomphe with Alex, his new little friend.

Like the previous day, he rang the doorbell. There was no answer. One minute passed, another, and then another. No response.

Slightly bewildered, he proceeded to the secret entrance that Alex had showed him the day before.

As he entered, his face grew pale. Broken glass, shards of metal, and a variance of wires littered Alex's backyard. The door to the shed hung open and the only window was broken.

Worried about his friend, Jeff made him way to the shed.

What he saw not only horrified him, but made him feel sick. Alex's computer screen had been ripped out of the circuits. His giant speaker had been crushed to pieces. All that remained was the portal. Examining the scene, Jeff found a note.

Jeff,

If you ever want to see your little friend Alex again, step into the portal. Bring no weapons and come alone. Bring the key, or else.

You have 48 hours.

Go.

- D

Confused as ever, Jeff sat down to collect his thoughts. *What key? Who is this D person?* He didn't remember Alex mentioning any *key* or any enemies. Terrified and lost, Jeff dropped to the floor and started sulking.

His green shirt became a musty olive as his sweat and tears drenched into it. His jeans became filthy with the dust and dirt that littered the floor of the shed.

Jeff had finally made a friend and now his friend was missing. He finally found something that excited him and now it was ruining his life.

After wallowing in sorrow, Jeff took a deep breath and began thinking. He searched the shed and suddenly, a glimmer of gold caught his eye. It was something stuck in the floor between a few planks of wood.

Jeff began digging and ripping the planks off. Then he saw it. It was a small golden flash drive labeled "Key."

Without having to wander anymore, Jeff knew what this *key* meant. He remembered Alex wanting to show him a surprise. Something about keeping a secret. Something about fixing a bug. Perhaps this was the key. The key to fixing the bug and making his portal into Minecraft work properly.

Without wasting another second, Jeff ran and hailed a cab. He had no time to waste waiting for a bus. He got home and began researching everything about Minecraft.

He had 48 hours to learn everything and rescue his friend Alex before something horrible would take place…

Printed in Great Britain
by Amazon.co.uk, Ltd.,
Marston Gate.

Printed in Great Britain
by Amazon.co.uk, Ltd.,
Marston Gate.